Family Story Collection

Nothing Is More Important Than Family

STORIES ABOUT FAMILY, LOVE, AND FRIENDSHIP

Book One

Book One

---⊗⊗⊗---

Nothing Is More Important Than Family

---⊗⊗⊗---

STORIES ABOUT FAMILY, LOVE, AND FRIENDSHIP

Introduction

The first love a child experiences is the love of his or her family—a mother's kiss, a father's hug, or a grandparent's undivided attention. A family's love is essential in helping a child learn how to give, as well as receive, love. It is the foundation upon which self-esteem, kindness, and compassion are built.

In "Letting Go," the Beast learns to put Belle's needs above his own, even when it hurts him. And in "Tigger Finds a Family," Tigger wishes for nothing more than a family to call his own. He soon realizes that families come in many different forms and sometimes good friends are all the family a person needs.

Letting Go

from *Beauty and the Beast*

True love means putting someone else's happiness above your own.

In order to break the spell that had turned him into a monster and his servants into enchanted objects, the Beast had to learn to love someone and to earn her love in return. But time was quickly running out.

The servants hoped Belle would be the one to break the spell. The Beast had taken her prisoner, but lately a friendship had begun to blossom between the two.

"I've never felt this way about anyone,"
the Beast told his servants after spending the
afternoon playing in the snow with Belle.
"I want to do something special for her.
But what?"

Lumiere the candelabrum gave the Beast the perfect idea. It would take a lot of planning to get the surprise ready for Belle, but the Beast knew it would make her happy.

Later that day, the Beast led Belle into the hallway and told her to close her eyes. Since the Beast was now her friend and Belle trusted him, she did. Then, the Beast took her into a glorious library with shelves and shelves of books, stacked from floor to ceiling.

"I can't believe it! This is wonderful." Belle cried when she opened her eyes. Belle loved reading—it was the perfect surprise! "Oh, thank you so much!"

The Beast smiled at Belle.

That evening, to help Belle and the Beast get even closer, the servants arranged a

romantic dinner for the pair. They both
dressed in their finest clothes and shared a
wonderful meal together.

Afterward, they sat on the terrace underneath
a canopy of stars. "Belle," the Beast asked softly,
"are you happy here with me?"

"Yes!" she exclaimed at once. But then her face grew sad, and she glanced away.

"What is it?" asked the Beast.

"If only I could see my father again—just for a moment," she said. "I miss him so much."

The Beast had an idea. "There is a way. . . ."

The Beast handed Belle a magic mirror. He told her it would show her anything she wanted to see.

When Belle's father appeared in the mirror, Belle gasped. "Papa! Oh, no!" she cried. "He's sick and all alone!"

The Beast could feel her pain as if it were his own. "You must go to him," he said. "I release you. You're no longer my prisoner."

"You mean I'm free?" Belle was amazed. "Oh, thank you!" She then spoke into the mirror, hoping her father could hear her. "Hold on, Papa! I'm on my way!"

As Belle rushed from the room, Cogsworth the mantel clock entered.

"I let her go," the Beast told him.

"You what?" Cogsworth exclaimed in dismay. "How could you do that? You'll stay a beast forever!"

"I had to," the Beast said, gazing after Belle. "I love her."

The Beast had finally learned to love another. In doing so, he realized something important: he would rather see Belle happy than keep her against her will—even if it meant he was doomed to remain a beast forever.

Tigger Finds a Family

from *The Tigger Movie*

Sometimes the love you're looking for is right under your whiskers.

Normally, Tigger liked to sing, "The most wonderful thing about tiggers is that I'm the only one!" Today, however, being the only one was making Tigger feel lonely, not wonderful.

Roo saw how sad Tigger was and tried to comfort him. Maybe there *were* other tiggers out there, Roo suggested. Roo had his mother, Kanga, so why shouldn't Tigger have a family, too?

"Can you imaginate it?" Tigger said to Roo. "More tiggers! And we'd all be bouncin'!"

Tigger and Roo wandered all through the woods, calling out, "Halloo! Tigger family!" but no one answered back. Tigger and Roo decided they needed to try something else.

So, they wrote a letter to the other tiggers

of the world. They mailed the letter and anxiously awaited a reply.

It didn't take long before Tigger got discouraged. "Why am I kiddin' myself?" he said sadly. "There aren't any other tiggers."

The next day, all of Tigger's friends gathered together. They hated to see Tigger so sad. Owl had an idea. "Young Roo," he said, "if you suggest that a letter will bring cheer to our friend Tigger, then we shall, by all means, write one."

It was easy to pretend to be Tigger's family because they all loved him so much. "Dress warmly," wrote Kanga. "Eat well," added Pooh. "Stay safe and keep smiling," wrote Piglet and Eeyore. And finally, Roo closed the letter with, "We're always there for you."

The next morning, when Tigger received the letter, he was overjoyed. But there was one problem: Tigger thought that his family was going to visit him. He even had a locket ready to fill with a family portrait. The friends knew they should tell Tigger the truth, but nobody had the heart to break the bad news to him.

Instead, they dressed up like tiggers and showed up at Tigger's house. But Tigger wasn't fooled for long. And when he realized what they had done, he felt lonelier than ever.

Tigger went off into the woods by himself and read his letter over and over.

"But . . . I thought you were always there for me," he said, as the letter slipped through his hands and blew away.

A little while later, Tigger heard his name being called. He looked down and thought his tigger family had finally arrived, but then he saw it was just his old friends. Tigger was so focused on finding other tiggers that he didn't see the family that was right in front of his eyes.

Tigger's friends took him home, but he still seemed sad. He wished his letter hadn't blown away. So his friends recited the words they had written.

"You mean you fellas are my family?" Tigger asked. "I shoulda seen it all along!" Tigger smiled. Then he opened his locket and placed a picture of his friends inside.